D1366046

This edition published in 1985 by Modern Publishing, a Division of
Unisystems, Inc. New York, NY 10022

Honey Bear Books® is a trademark owned by Honey Bear Productions, Inc. and is registered in the
U.S. Patent and Trademark office. All rights reserved.

ISBN 0-87449-036-7 Copyright© 1985 by Victoria House Publishing Ltd.

All rights reserved. No part of this publication may be reproduced, stored in a retrieval system, or
transmitted, in any form or by any means, electronic, mechanical, photocopying, recording or other-
wise, without the permission of the copyright holders or Modern Publishing.

Printed in Brazil

LITTLE MOUSE'S
BEDTIME STORIES

MODERN PUBLISHING
A Division of Unisystems, Inc.
New York, New York 10022

Contents

LITTLE
MOUSE'S
BEDTIME
STORIES

The Telescope

It was a rainy day. It had poured since breakfast without stopping. Little Bunny stared out the window.

"I'm bored," said Benny. "What shall we do?"

"I know," said Little Bunny, jumping. "Why don't we go exploring?"

"We'd get wet," grumbled Benny.

"I don't mean *outside*. Let's explore *inside*. There are lots and lots of passages leading from our burrow."

They borrowed their father's flashlight to light their way.

The passage got dustier and narrower as they went along. Soon Benny called out, "Look!" and shined the light on a door in the wall of the passage.

The handle was hard to turn, but they managed it and the door creaked open slowly. Benny and Little Bunny could hardly see in the dark, but they could just make out some chairs and boxes. As their eyes got used to the darkness, they saw all sorts of other things—bottles, candlesticks, old paintings, a trombone, and a marble statue. Everything was covered in a

thick layer of dust as though no one had been there for ages.

In a corner they found a big wooden box. Inside were a lot of old maps and a shiny gold tube with glass ends.

"What do you think this is?" asked Benny.

Little Bunny shook his head. "Let's ask Daddy."

"I haven't seen that old thing for years," he said, very pleased. "It belonged to my grandfather, Silas. He was a sea captain and he sailed to lots of faraway places. I'll tell you all about his adventures one day."

"Oh, please," said Little Bunny. "But what *is* it?"

9

"It's a telescope. You look through one end and it makes faraway things look closer. Grandfather used it at sea to search for land. You can use it at night to see the stars. It's stopped raining, so we could try it later."

Mr. Bunny told an exciting story of how Silas Bunny sailed through a terrible storm. Then he took them outside to look at the stars through the telescope.

"How beautiful," said Benny. "I never noticed them."

"Come on," said Mr. Bunny. "Time for bed. We'll use the telescope another day."

"All right," said Little Bunny. "Maybe we'll have great adventures one day, too!"

The Billberry Ghost

One spring morning the playground at school was filled with noise and excitement. There were to be no lessons that day. They were going on a school trip.

The bus came and they all scrambled on. Soon they were driving through open countryside, past fields and a river, until, at last, they climbed up a steep hill on top of which stood Billberry Museum.

"This museum used to be a huge house," said Mr. Mole.

"The Billberry Bunnys lived here years ago," he said. "We are in the Great Hall where they held parties with dancing and music that lasted a week. Let's go up to the bedrooms and see the old beds that they once slept in."

"What funny beds!" said Little Squirrel. "They've got curtains around them."

"I think it's a good idea," said Willie Woodpecker. "They must be warm in winter."

"They're very lumpy," announced Little Owl.

"You aren't supposed to climb on them," said Mr. Mole.

Next they visited a room filled with old swords and suits of armor.

"The Billberrys collected armor," said Mr. Mole. "Imagine what it was like wearing heavy iron suits like this."

They saw the garden and then it was time to go.

Everyone hurried back to the bus. Mr. Mole stood by the door and counted them as they got in.

"We're one short," he said when everyone had sat down. "Who's missing?"

"It's Willie," called Little Owl. "Willie's missing."

"Little Mouse, would you mind going back to get him?" asked Mr. Mole.

Little Mouse ran back into the museum.

A few minutes later she returned running as fast as she could, quite out of breath, and without Willie.

"G-g-ghost! I've seen a ghost!" she cried. "It was wearing a suit of armor—just like the ones we saw."

"We'd all better look for Willie," said Mr. Mole.

They walked slowly into the museum. As they got near one room, they heard a noise. Little Mouse peeped in the door and saw a suit of armor shaking from side to side and rattling loudly. Mr. Mole suddenly laughed.

"That's no ghost!" he said, and walked right up to the shaking figure.

He lifted the helmet and there was Willie trying hard to get out of the suit of armor that he had tried on!

Little Owl's Garden

Little Owl had always wanted a flower garden of his own, but his father liked growing vegetables better. Whenever Little Owl planted a few flowers they seemed to get covered up by cabbages or crushed by squash.

He had pretty much given up growing things until one spring when there was a very windy spell.

"It sounds terrible out there tonight," Mrs. Owl said one evening. "I'm worried about that shaky chimney pot."

"I'll fly up and check it in the morning," said Mr. Owl.

But there was a big crash in the night and Mrs. Owl knew that the chimney pot had fallen down.

The next morning Little Owl went out to look. There was the chimney pot right in the middle of Mr. Owl's garden and it hadn't so much as squashed a Brussels sprout.

"That was lucky," said Mr. Owl. "I don't think we'll put that

old pot back. I'll buy a new one today."

While Mr. Owl was out, Little Owl had an idea.

"Don't you think the chimney pot would look good where it is, filled with flowers?" he asked his mother.

"That's a wonderful idea!" said Mrs. Owl. "Flowers would brighten up that green vegetable patch beautifully."

So Little Owl filled the chimney pot with dirt and planted some bright pansies in the top of it. He didn't worry about his flowers getting covered up or squashed because they were way above the vegetables, safe in their chimney pot garden.

The Big Catch

"It's too hot to do anything!" moaned Nippy Shrew.

"Why don't we go fishing?" suggested Little Bunny. "It will be cool by the stream."

"Good idea!" said Nippy, and he ran home to get his rod.

Soon they were sitting under the willow trees beside the stream. They could see fish jumping all around them, but not one came near their fishing lines.

"Fishing's boring," said Little Bunny, who was tired of waiting for something to happen. "Why don't we..."

Just then he felt a tug on his line and he almost went head-over-heels into the water.

"Quick, Nippy!" he shouted. "Give me a hand." They both pulled as hard as they could.

"It must be a big one!" said Little Bunny excitedly. They pulled again and suddenly they fell backwards.

They couldn't believe their eyes. They hadn't caught a fish—they had hooked an old kettle, full of holes.

"This is great!" said Nippy. "It's just what I need."

"Don't be silly! What can you do with an old kettle?"

"Come to my house this afternoon and you'll find out," answered Nippy. "And bring your bathing suit."

As Little Bunny walked up to Nippy's house later, he heard a lot of splashing. There was Nippy standing under a lovely shower of water!

"Don't you like my shower?" he asked. Nippy had hung the old kettle from a tree and put a hose inside. Water poured from all the holes in the kettle.

"Neat!" said Little Bunny, jumping under the water. "This is the best way to spend a hot afternoon."

Locked Out

Mrs. Bunny was baking. She had made four loaves of bread, a walnut cake, a carrot and banana pie, and a big batch of rolls.

"It is hot in this kitchen," said Mrs. Bunny, as she put the last rolls in the oven. "I'll just go out into the garden for some fresh air while these are baking."

She was chatting with Mrs. Hoppit when there was a gust of wind and bang! Mrs. Bunny's front door blew shut.

"Oh no!" she cried. "I'm locked out and my rolls will be burned if I don't get back in quickly!"

A small window was open, but Mrs. Bunny couldn't fit through. Mrs. Hoppit tried, but she was too big as well.

"What are you doing?" called Mrs. Mouse. When they explained, she tried to climb through the window, but she couldn't squeeze through either.

"You'll have to call the fire department," she said. "I was going that way so I'll stop in and tell them."

"Thank you," said Mrs. Bunny. "Oh, my poor rolls!"

"What's the matter, Mrs. Bunny?" called Willie Woodpecker, who was on his way home from school.

Willie tried the window, but his shape was wrong. Little Squirrel was walking by so she tried, and soon Little Bunny and Tootie Owl arrived. No one could get inside.

Just then Little Mouse came by.

"If anyone can do it, Little Mouse can," said Willie.

But Little Mouse was too big. Mrs. Bunny began to cry.

"My poor rolls will be burned to cinders. And if the firemen don't get here soon, the oven may catch fire too. Then our nice little house will burn down."

Mrs. Bunny was sobbing when the fire engine arrived.

"Don't worry, Mrs. Bunny," said the fireman kindly. "Just dry your eyes and then we'll see what we can do."

Mrs. Bunny reached into her pocket and pulled out her handkerchief. As she did, something fell to the ground.

"Look!" cried Little Bunny. "It's the front-door key! It was in your pocket all the time!"

Everyone burst into laughter and Mrs. Bunny felt very uneasy. But she soon cheered up. The rolls weren't burned—they were just ready to eat, nice and hot from the oven, and everyone enjoyed them.

The Easter Egg Hunt

"Let's have an Easter egg hunt this year," suggested Little Owl at school one day. "We'll hide eggs all over the woods and then we'll look for them."

"Good idea," said Little Squirrel. "You be in charge."

Little Owl was thrilled to be in charge. He collected money from everyone to pay for the eggs and a few days before the hunt he went to the grocery store.

"Do you have any candy eggs that we can use for our hunt?" asked Little Owl.

Mrs. Badger had jars filled with tiny Easter eggs. Little Owl chose chocolate eggs and she wrapped them up.

"I must put them in a safe place," he thought on the way home. "Somewhere I won't be tempted to eat them."

On the morning of the hunt, Little Owl finished his breakfast as quickly as he could.

"Before you hide your eggs, please wind the clock," Mrs. Owl said. "It will stop if it isn't wound soon."

But Little Owl wasn't really listening. He was trying to remember where he'd put the eggs. He looked in the cabinets and in the closets but the eggs weren't there.

He was still looking when his friends arrived. Poor Little Owl couldn't tell them he'd lost the eggs.

They would probably think that he had eaten them!

"Can we start hunting?" asked Little Mouse excitedly.

"Um. Er, yes, I suppose so," said Little Owl, who couldn't think of what to do.

He sat down and watched them all searching for eggs.

"Oh dear," he thought miserably. "They're bound to find out soon. Whatever will I say?"

He thought about hiding somewhere but just then Little Bunny ran up.

"Where are all the eggs?" he asked. "I haven't found one—and neither has anyone else. I think it's a trick!"

Then they all began shouting, "Where are the eggs? Where are the eggs?" Little Owl was just wishing he could make himself invisible when a voice called out to him. It was Mrs. Owl, and she sounded angry.

"I asked you to wind the clock this morning, but you forgot and now it's stopped. You'd better set it now."

"I can't do anything right today," thought Little Owl.

As he opened the clock, he saw a big bag.

"The eggs! I've found the eggs!" he shouted and ran out to his friends, who were glad to finally see them.

Everyone decided there had been enough hunting, so they just shared the eggs and enjoyed them.

When Mrs. Owl heard what happened, she laughed and said, "It's a good thing you didn't put them inside the grandfather clock. That only needs winding once a year!"

The Painting Trip

One afternoon, Mr. Mole took the class on a painting trip. They found a nice sunny spot where they could do nature paintings.

"You can paint whatever you like," Mr. Mole told them.

Little Mouse saw a butterfly and thought it would make a great picture. She took out her paints very quietly so she wouldn't disturb it.

She was doing very well, but then the butterfly flew off. Taking her paints, Little Mouse ran after it.

It landed on a big rose bush and poor Little Mouse got very prickled in the rose garden.

She colored in one wing and then the butterfly flew off again, this time up to the branch of a tree.

"Oh dear," said Little Mouse as she climbed up. "It isn't very easy painting up a tree."

But the butterfly was soon off again so fast that Little

Mouse had to run so she didn't lose sight of it.

Racing ahead, she didn't notice when her feet began to sink into the soft ground. Suddenly, she fell flat on her face into an enormous puddle of mud.

Wiping the mud from her eyes, she looked around for the butterfly but it was nowhere to be seen. Poor Little Mouse! She took her half-finished painting and went back to join the others.

Mr. Mole laughed kindly when he saw her covered with mud. "You look like a nature painting yourself!" he told her. "Such hard work deserves a special prize!"

Back at school, Mr. Mole gave Little Mouse a beautiful picture of a butterfly just like the one she had been painting.

Little Mouse was so pleased. She finished her picture and hung the two butterflies side by side in her bedroom.

Little Owl's Birthday Surprise

Little Owl yawned and stretched. He tried to remember why today was special. Of course! It was his birthday.

He leapt out of bed and raced down to the kitchen. But no one was there. He went all through the house. He was all alone on his birthday! He went next door, to the Squirrels.

"Mrs. Squirrel!" he called, but no one was there either. "What an awful birthday!" thought Little Owl sadly. "I guess I'll go to my favorite place—the old oak tree."

As he flew toward it, he noticed something big and square and brown built on the lower branches.

"Why it's a tree house!" he cried. "Who's built a house in *my* tree? I'll certainly find out!"

He poked his head angrily around the door. There they all were—Mr. and Mrs. Owl, his sister Tootie, and the Squirrel family.

"Surprise!" they cried. "Happy birthday, Little Owl!"

"But whose house is this?" asked Little Owl, puzzled.

"It's yours," said Mr. Owl. "Your own tree house!"

"Yippee!" shouted Little Owl. "I'm not having such a bad birthday after all!"

The Party Dress

Every summer there was a big party in town. All the trees were decorated with flowers and lit by glow worms. The Rambling Mousekins band played their flutes and there was dancing until dawn—or until the band fell asleep.

Little Squirrel tried on her special party dress.

"It's no good," said Mrs. Squirrel. "You've outgrown it. I really don't have time to make you a new one so you'll just have to wear your everyday dress."

Little Squirrel ran out of the house. She went all the way to the stream and sat down and cried miserably.

"Whatever's the matter with you?" asked Mrs. Duck.

Little Squirrel explained and Mrs. Duck said, "Come with me." She led the way to her house in the reeds.

"Now let's see what we've got," said Mrs. Duck, opening a big wooden chest in the corner.

Little Squirrel was amazed to see all the feathers that spilled out of it—blue ones, green ones, beautiful brown ones, fluffy ones, long shiny ones—all sorts.

"Which colors do you like best?" asked Mrs. Duck. "You'll be the only one at the party in a feather dress, I'll bet."

Little Squirrel chose blue and green. She helped Mrs. Duck sew the feathers together. It was quite easy once she knew how.

At last the dress was ready.

"Try it on," said Mrs. Duck. "There's the mirror," she laughed, pointing to the stream.

"Oh! It's . . . beautiful! Thank

you so much," said Little Squirrel, dancing on the bank.

It was the best party Little Squirrel could remember. She was chosen as Woodland Princess and she danced until she fell asleep and her father carried her home.

Uncle Monty's Mystery

"Uncle Monty is coming to visit," Mrs. Mouse told Little Mouse. "I'll be very busy, so I want you to spend some time with him," she said.

When Uncle Monty arrived, he looked very serious.

"Oh dear, this isn't going to be fun," Little Mouse thought. But she tried to make Uncle Monty welcome and gave him a big glass of iced tea.

She showed Uncle Monty the town park, and her friend's

homes. But he didn't say much and nothing seemed to make him very happy.

Then they saw Nippy Shrew, Little Bunny and Little Owl.

"Hello," called Little Mouse. "This is my Uncle Monty, who is visiting us." They stared up at the strict-looking man. But Uncle Monty smiled and asked Little Mouse to run home to fetch his shiny brown case. "I have something to show you," he told them mysteriously.

Little Mouse was so surprised to see Uncle Monty smiling that she ran home as fast as she could and ran all the way back with the case!

When Uncle Monty opened his case, Little Mouse was amazed to see a big top hat, white gloves, a silver wand and lots of strange boxes and packages.

Uncle Monty put on the gloves and hat, tapped his wand and began to do all sorts of magic tricks. Soon a big crowd gathered to watch Uncle Monty's special Magic Show.

Little Mouse was very proud of her uncle.

"Thank you, Uncle Monty," she whispered.

"Thank *you*, Little Mouse," he said. "Your friends were great! I haven't enjoyed myself so much for years!"

And with a smile, he popped the big top hat on Little Mouse's head and let her wear it all the way home.

Mrs. Prickles Sees A Ghost

Little Owl, Nippy Shrew and Tom Prickles were playing tag. After a while, they felt tired and sat down on the grass.

"I'm starving," said Nippy.

"Let's get a snack," said Tom. "We'll slip into my Mom's bakery and see if there are any cinnamon rolls."

As they crept through the kitchen door, they could hear Mrs. Prickles talking to a customer in the shop.

"I'll get you some rolls from the kitchen," she said.

"Quick, hide!" cried Tom. He and Little Owl crawled under a table. Nippy jumped into a big barrel.

Mrs. Prickles went back into the shop. Tom and Little Owl came out and looked all around for Nippy.

"Where are you, Nippy?" whispered Tom.

Suddenly, the flour bin opened and a ghostly white figure appeared. It was Nippy, covered from head to toe in flour. Tom jumped in surprise.

"Aaagh!" screamed Little Owl and he and Tom ran off—just as Mrs. Prickles rushed in. She screamed, too, and ran into the shop shouting, "I've seen a ghost!"

Nippy hopped out of the barrel, shook off all the flour, took cinnamon rolls for everyone, and ran outside. When he explained what had happened they laughed and laughed.

Mrs. Prickles never found out what happened, but she still enjoys telling customers about the ghost that ate six of her delicious cinnamon rolls.

The Lookalikes

Cousin Katie had come to visit Little Squirrel.

"Well, well," said Mrs. Squirrel, looking at the two cousins, "you two almost look like twin squirrels!"

It was true. When they looked in the mirror, they could hardly tell the difference themselves! Their noses, eyes, and long bushy tails were almost identical.

"We could play a trick on my friends," said Little Squirrel, whispering her plan into Katie's ear.

Later that afternoon in the woods, Little Squirrel sent Katie to hide behind a tree and went to join her friends in their game of hide-and-seek.

When it was Little Squirrel's turn to hide, she hid behind a tree on the opposite side of the clearing from Katie. Then, just as they'd planned, Katie waved and shouted, "Here I am!" Everyone ran toward her.

A minute later, Little Squirrel popped out from the other tree. "No—over here!" she cried.

Her friends turned around in amazement. How could Little Squirrel be in *two* places at once?

By this time, Katie had run to another hiding place. She poked her head out, calling, "Yoo hoo, here I am!"

Everyone looked puzzled. "Just how many Little Squirrels are there today?" asked Little Mouse, confused.

"Only one!" laughed Little Squirrel as she ran over. "This is my cousin Katie who looks just like me."

Everyone thought it was a good joke, but they agreed with Benny Bunny that *one* Little Squirrel was enough!

The Egg And Spoon Race

School Sports Day was always fun. There were lots of contests but everybody's favorite was the egg-and-spoon race. Little Bunny usually took home quite a few prizes because he was good at running, but he never won that race.

"My egg always falls off," he told Little Squirrel.

"Well, you just have to keep trying," said Little Squirrel kindly. "Stick to it."

"That's it!" shouted Little Bunny excitedly.

"What?" asked Little Squirrel, looking surprised.

"Oh, nothing," answered Little Bunny and he ran home.

On Sports Day, when it was time for the egg-and-spoon race, all the runners lined up and Mr. Mole shouted, "Go!"

They couldn't run very fast because they had to keep their eggs from falling off the spoons. Little Owl lost his egg right away, but Little Bunny seemed to run like the wind and finished well ahead of the others.

"I won!" he shouted and waved his spoon in the air.

"Be careful!" called Mr. Owl, who was standing nearby. "If you wave your spoon like that the egg will drop off."

But Little Bunny didn't hear. He tossed his spoon up high and caught it. The egg was still on the spoon.

"Let me look at that spoon," said Mr. Owl.

He took the spoon and tired to lift the egg. He couldn't. It was glued on. Little Bunny went red.

Mr. Mole marched over and told Little Bunny there would

be no prizes for him that day. Little Bunny went home with drooping ears.

"I'll never cheat again," he told Benny. "Next year I'll practice and win the egg-and-spoon race—honestly!"

Trick or Treat

It was Halloween and Mr. Mole was reading ghost stories to the class.

"Now," he said, "I want *you* to write about Halloween."

After lunch, they all read their stories. They had fun hearing about made-up witches and monsters.

"Do you think there really are ghosts and witches?" Little Squirrel asked Little Mouse.

"No! They're only in stories," said Little Mouse.

But when she walked home from school that day, she couldn't help wishing it wasn't quite so dark under the trees.

"Thank goodness I'm nearly home," she thought. But suddenly she saw a strange orange head coming toward her. It was glowing and smiling. Little Mouse screamed and ran as fast as she could inside her house.

"I saw a...a...monster!" she told her mother.

Mrs. Mouse didn't seem worried. "It's Halloween," she said. "Everyone thinks they see things on Halloween."

Just then there was a knock at the door. Little Mouse opened the door, gave a loud scream, and shut it quickly.

"Whatever is the matter?" asked Mrs. Mouse.

"The monster knocked at the door," cried Little Mouse.

Mrs. Mouse smiled. "I think we should let it in, then. It might want something to eat," she said.

"No," cried Little Mouse, hiding behind her mother.

Then Little Mouse looked. The monster was really a big carved pumpkin with a nightlight inside to make it glow!

"Hello!" said Timmy, who was holding the pumpkin. "that was a good trick, wasn't it?"

"No," said Little Mouse, who was angry that her brother's trick had worked so well.

"Your 'monster' has helped me make a special treat," said Mrs. Mouse. "It's pumpkin pie!"

"My favorite!" said Little Mouse, grinning, and Timmy's pumpkin lantern grinned back.

Little Owl's Hiccups

"Hic!" went Little Owl at breakfast one morning.

"Oh dear," said Mrs. Owl. "You've got hiccups. Drink a glass of water."

Little Owl tried that but he still kept hiccuping.

"Try the wrong side of the glass," said Mr. Owl.

Little Owl tried that and spilled water all over himself, so he had to go and change. Mrs. Owl got angry with Mr. Owl for suggesting something so silly.

"At least it worked," he said, but Little Owl came back into the kitchen and went "Hic!" once again.

"Hold your nose while you drink," said Tootie.

"If I drink much more water I'll burst," said Little Owl, but he tried it anyway. It didn't work.

"I can't go to school with hiccups," he said.

"You can't stay at home for something like that," said Mrs. Owl.

"You'll have to get rid of them on the way."

Little Owl started for school and asked everyone he met if they knew a cure for hiccups. They *all* did!

"Stand on your head," said Little Bunny.

"Hold your breath and count," said Little Squirrel.

"Put an acorn down your back," said Willie Woodpecker.

Little Owl tried all the ideas but none of them worked.

"It'll be just awful if I hiccup all day," thought Little Owl, as he went into the classroom.

"Good morning," said Mr. Mole. "You all wrote stories last night for homework. Today I'd like you to read them to the class. Stand up, Little Owl, and you can begin."

What a shock for Little Owl! He had forgotten all about his homework and had nothing to read. Of course, Mr. Mole wasn't very pleased and he said Little Owl had to stay in at playtime to write his story.

"Cheer up, Little Owl," whispered Tootie. "At least your hiccups are gone. A big shock is the best cure!"

Little Bunny Helps Out

One day Little Bunny asked his mother if he could help her clean the house. Mrs. Bunny gave him a small brush so he could work beside her.

As Mrs. Bunny went by the window she saw Mrs. Squirrel walking by. "I'm going to speak to Mrs. Squirrel," she told Little Bunny. "We'll do the dishes when I come back."

Little Bunny thought to himself, "I'll wash the dishes myself. That will be a surprise for Mommy!"

Little Bunny got a stool so he could reach the faucet.

First he squeezed the dishwashing liquid into the sink. He wasn't sure how much to use, so he added a little more—and then more again. Then he turned the faucet on all the way. As the water spurted into the sink, the soap quickly turned into mounds of fluffy suds.

They spilled onto the floor and even started foaming up around the stool that Little Bunny was standing on! He finally felt the faucet through the suds and turned it off.

"Oh no!" cried Little Bunny. "What am I going to do? Mommy will be angry—the kitchen is all bubbly!"

Then he had an idea.

He opened the window above the sink. Then he opened the door too. A breeze blew into the room, and the suds and bubbles began to rise and drift out of the window.

Mrs. Bunny was talking to Mrs. Squirrel when she saw a strange sight above her house. "Look!" she said, pointing to the sky, "hundreds of bubbles with the sun shining on them! I wonder where they came from?"

They watched bubbles float like a cloud and then scatter in the air.

When Mrs. Bunny came in, Little Bunny had everything in the kitchen back to normal. What a narrow escape!

"Will you help with the dishes now?" asked Mrs. Bunny.

Little Bunny just smiled and nodded his head as one last tiny bubble glistened on the end of his whiskers.

The Amazing Talking Snowman

One morning Little Mouse woke up and looked out of her window to see that it had been snowing all night.

"Timmy, it's snowing!" she cried, running into his room and waking him up. "Let's make a snowman!"

They dressed quickly and were busily scooping snow into a big pile when Timmy had an idea.

"Let's make a special snowman. We'll make it talk!"

Little Mouse didn't see how they could make a snowman talk, but Timmy had soon set up his trick.

"It'll surprise our friends," he said as they gave the snowman a hat, a carrot nose and two chestnuts for eyes.

Just then Little Owl walked past and Timmy decided to try out the snowman.

"You call him into the yard. I'll make the snowman talk," he whispered to Little Mouse.

Little Owl laughed when Little Mouse explained about the talking snowman, but he said he'd look. As he walked up to it, the snowman spoke in a deep, hollow voice.

"It really does talk!" he cried, and he began to ask it questions until it was time to go to school.

In class, Little Owl told everyone about the snowman. They all asked Little Mouse if they could see it and she told them to come right after school.

It was a lovely sunny day as they tramped back to Little Mouse's house. Timmy ran ahead to get ready to play his trick. He dashed around the house to wait.

Soon everyone was gathered around the snowman, whispering and giggling with excitement.

"Hello," said the snowman slowly. But just then Benny Bunny pointed and cried, "The snowman's melting!"

The snowman *was* melting, very quickly—and so was the snow on the ground. And, as it did, they all noticed Mr. Mouse's green garden hose, leading from the snowman's mouth all the way around the side of the house.

They followed the hose to where Timmy Mouse was talking through it, pretending to be the snowman. Poor Timmy was found out! Everyone teased him for a long time afterward about the amazing, *melting* snowman.